For Jolyon – J.N.H.
For Daniel – L.R.

First published in Great Britain and in the USA in 2006 by Frances Lincoln Children's Books,
4 Torriano Mews, Torriano Avenue, London NW5 2RZ

www.franceslincoln.com

Distributed in the USA by Publishers Group West

British Library Cataloguing in Publication Data available on request

ISBN 1-84507-127-1

The illustrations are acryllic paint and coloured pencil

Set in Today

Printed in China
1 3 5 7 9 8 6 4 2

I can do it!

Jana Novotny Hunter

Illustrated by

Lucy Richards

FRANCES LINCOLN CHILDREN'S BOOKS

Everybody can do things in different ways –
mummies, daddies, and babies too!
We can do things in lots of ways...

especially me and you!

Today I'm off to nursery. I eat up all my breakfast
and it makes my legs speed up.

So I can be...

Nutmeg Nursery

fast

Phew! After that zoom-zooming about, my legs need a rest.

So now I use my paws.

I can roll my playdough,

Yes!

and pound, pound, pound it hard into whatever shape I want!

I can be...

STRONG

I can choose things by myself too –
things to stick on my picture!

I choose
a soft feather,

a button,

some glitter,

and a floaty ribbon.

I don't make a sound.

Because I can be...

I've got lots more work to do today.
So when my picture's finished,
I get on with...

digging,

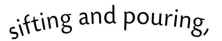
sifting and pouring,

and piling up sand.

Scrabble, scrabble,

my paws just don't stop!

There's such a lot to do! So I can be...

Then I get out
the building bricks.

Building

is very

w-wobbly

work!

I have
to build
my tower
over...
and... over...
again.

But I can be...

carefully

All that careful building makes
me ready for some sounds.

So I bang, **bang**

a drum and the **BOOM**,

BA-BOOM, BANG

goes right up my arms.

LOUDER, LOUDER

till it hurts my ears!

Yes! I can be...

NOISY

My teacher thinks it's time
for Finding Out now,
and I like that.

I find out that magnets
suck up paperclips.

They stick to nails,

and scissors,

and keys,

but not to me!

I find that out because

I can be...

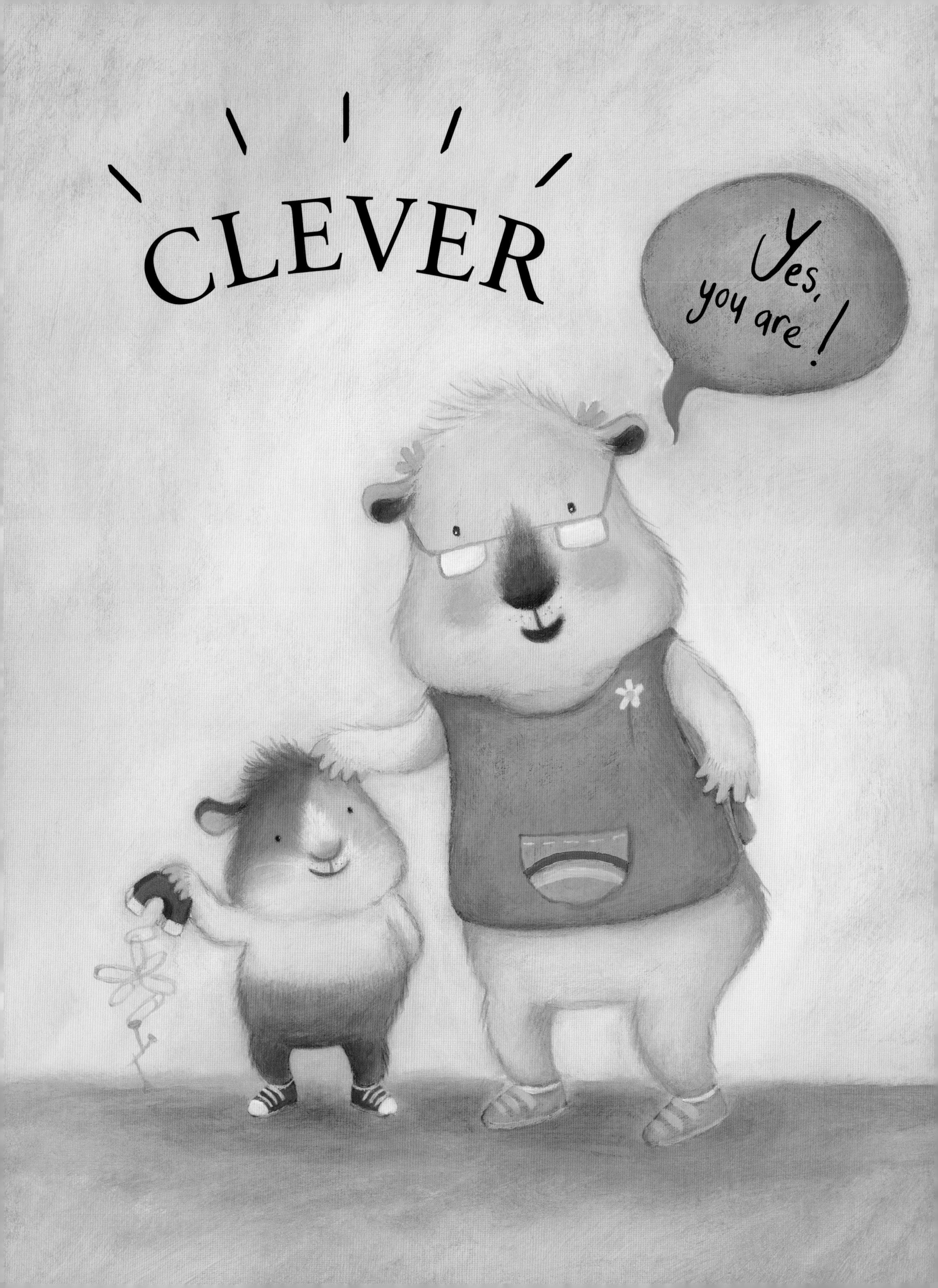
CLEVER
Yes, you are!

"Let's play the Bus Game!"
says Teacher.

So I put on
the driver's hat

and I line up

the chairs.

I ring the bell

and make the money go

clink clink

because that shows how

I can be...

helpful

But I **won't** be helpful
if I'm never the bus driver!

Then my teacher says
I can be her Helper.
She needs me to help her
get ready for Home Time.

So I show
how I can be
busy and **strong,**

careful
and
helpful,

and **quiet** and **clever** too.

Then I can be

noisy

and **fast**

as I run...

right into my mummy's arms!

Everybody can do things in different ways –
mummies, daddies, and babies too!
We can do things in lots of ways...

especially me and you!